KU-523-364

Mr Super Poopy Pants

34 4124 0010 3519

For Benjy, who truly is super x

Text and illustrations copyright © 2014 Rebecca Elliott
This edition copyright © 2014 Lion Hudson

The right of Rebecca Elliott to be identified as the author and illustrator of this work has been asserted by her in accordance with the Copyright, Designs and Patents Act 1988.

All rights reserved. No part of this publication may be reproduced or transmitted in any form or by any means, electronic or mechanical, including photocopy, recording, or any information storage and retrieval system, without permission in writing from the publisher.

Published by Lion Children's Books
an imprint of
Lion Hudson plc
Wilkinson House, Jordan Hill Road,
Oxford OX2 8DR, England
www.lionhudson.com/lionchildrens

Hardback ISBN 978 0 7459 6516 1
Paperback ISBN 978 0 7459 6465 2

First edition 2014

A catalogue record for this book is available from the British Library

Printed and bound in China, June 2014, LH06

Rebecca Elliott
MR SUPER POOPY PANTS
PP
LION
CHILDREN'S

First it was just me and my big sister, Clemmie.

But then Mummy got really huge.

And we were told we were getting a new baby brother.

I thought we could name him Batman and have adventures together.

I was wrong.

Instead his name is Benjamin. Or as I call him...

Mr Poopy Pants.

And he can't run around, invent gadgets,
OR fight crime.

He can't even talk yet. No matter what I do.

"APPLE," I say.
Nothing.

"BALL."

Nothing.

"CHONDROSTEOSAURUS."
Even less.

Instead he just sleeps,

cries,

dribbles,

parps,

burps,

and poops.

In his pants. **All the time.**

I've been studying him, and it turns out Mr Poopy Pants does several different kinds of poops.

Here are some of my favourites...

1. The Submarine Poop.

This causes widespread panic and is particularly funny when Daddy is giving us a bath.

2. The Ghost Poop.

He smells like he's pooped. He looks like he's pooped.
But he hasn't pooped.

Good for clearing an area of the park quickly when it's a bit busy.

3. The Waterfall Poop.

A poop able to escape even the strongest and biggest nappy.

Good for a speedy escape from a boring posh party.

So... actually Benjamin has some great super powers.

He is Super after all! He's a Pooperhero!

The amazing,
cuddly,
funny,
stinky...

MR
SUPER
POOPY PANTS

He flies through the air with his parp power, saving the world from boring baths, busy parks, and posh parties one poopy nappy bomb at a time.

He still can't talk yet though.
But I don't mind.

Clemmie can't talk either and she's excellent.

I can talk enough for the three of us.

"Night-night, Clemmie.
"Night-night, Mr Super Poopy Pants."

N-NIGHT TOBY!

Other titles from Rebecca Elliott

Just Because
Sometimes
Zoo Girl
The Last Tiger